This vacation Bible school inspired the
Bible Buddy named Decker. Decker
is a decorator crab. In God's creation,
decorator crabs are real makers who
bling out their shells with everything
from sand dollars to seashells.

How cool is that?

Best of Buddies
I Was Born for This!

Written by **JEFF WHITE**   *Illustrated by* **JOHN JAY CABUAY**

Copyright © 2017 Group Publishing, Inc./ISNI: 0000 0001 0362 4853
Lifetree is an imprint of Group Publishing, Inc.
group.com

Library of Congress Cataloging-in-Publications Data on file.

ISBN: 978-1-4707-4853-1 (Hard Cover)
ISBN: 978-1-4707-5023-7 (e Pub)
Printed in China. 001 CHINA 0617

10 9 8 7 6 5 4 3 2 1   21 20 19 18 17

Written by **JEFF WHITE**   Illustrated by **JOHN JAY CABUAY**

Decker loves to decorate. He paints. He spiffs up.

He sparkles. He adds beauty and charm.

Sometimes he even festoons!

Decker loves it!

"I was born for this," he says,

"because that's how
God made me!"

Decker decorates everything he sees.

When Decker sees a plain, boring chair,

he feels a tingle inside.

Should Decker decorate the chair?

Yes! "I was born for this!" Decker says.

He adds paint, ribbons, and glitter.

That's a chair with flair!

Now Decker spies a hat.

Just a normal, dull hat.

Should Decker decorate the hat?

Yes! "I was born for this!" Decker says.

He adds stripes, jewels, and some bells.

That thing SINGS!

Uh-oh. Decker sees a pizza. A bland, cheese pizza.

Should Decker decorate the pizza?

Yes! "I was born for this!" Decker says.

He adds colorful veggies and tiny fishies.

That's a pizza with pizzazz!

What does Decker see now?

He sees a cake. A white, humdrum cake.

Should Decker decorate the cake?

Yes! "I was born for this!" Decker says.

He makes it better with sprinkles,

candles, and polka dots.

That takes the cake!

What's that? Decker sees a table.

An empty, lonely table.

Should Decker decorate the table?

Yes! "I was born for this!" Decker says.

He adds the pizza, cake, and hats to the table.

He adds balloons, too!

Decker must be making something extra special.

Now Decker sees his friends walking by.

Should Decker decorate…his friends?

Um…no. But Decker is all ready for a party!

And he can decorate his party

with his friends!

Decker made a few things better…

and he made his friends happy.

"You were born for this!" they say.

Decker is happy, too.

"That's how God made me!" he says.